SpongeBob EXPOSED!

THE INSIDER'S GUIDE TO SpongeBob SquarePants

NICKELODEON

Based on the TV series *SpongeBob SquarePants*® created by Stephen Hillenburg

as seen on Nickelodeon®

SIMON SPOTLIGHT

An imprint of Simon & Schuster Children's Publishing Division

1230 Avenue of the Americas, New York, New York 10020

Manufactured in China

Designed by Giuseppe Castellano

The art on pages 8, 9, 11, 54-63, 84, 87, 89, 92, and 93 is illustrated by Gregg Schigiel.

First Edition

2 4 6 8 10 9 7 5 3 1

ISBN 0-689-86870-7

Library of Congress Catalog Card Number 2004104054

SpongeBob EXPOSED!

THE INSIDER'S GUIDE TO

by STEVEN BANKS

Simon Spotlight/Nickelodeon
New York London Toronto Sydney

TABLE of CONTENTS

THE MAN BEHIND THE NAUTICAL NONSENSE 8

MEET THE CAST! 12

DID YOU KNOW? WATERLOGGED TRIVIA 30

HOME SWEET HOMES! 34

WHO SAID WHAT? 42

WILL THE REAL SPONGEBOB PLEASE STAND UP? 44

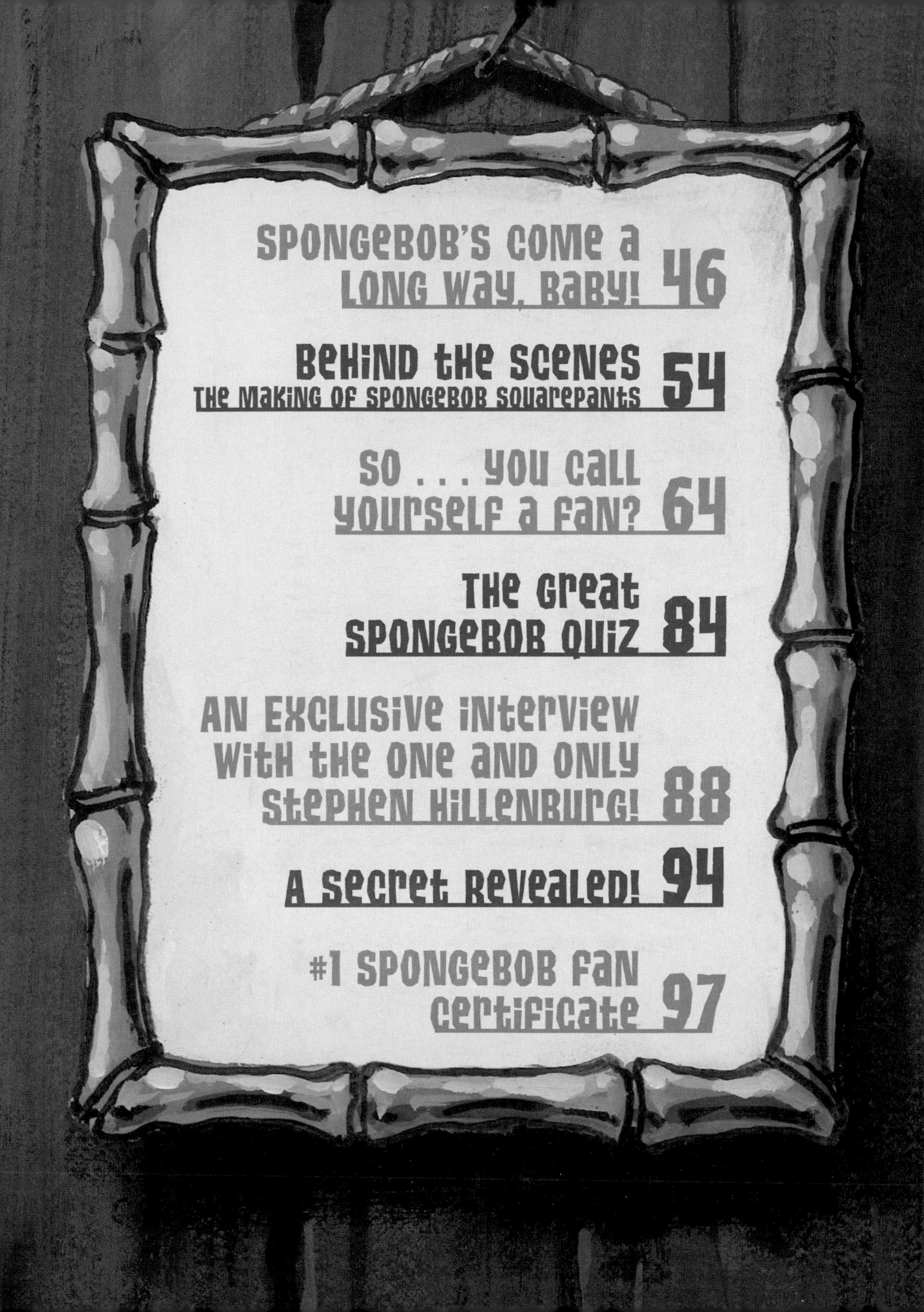

SPONGEBOB'S COME A LONG WAY, BABY! 46
BEHIND THE SCENES THE MAKING OF SPONGEBOB SQUAREPANTS 54
SO . . . YOU CALL YOURSELF A FAN? 64
THE GREAT SPONGEBOB QUIZ 84
AN EXCLUSIVE INTERVIEW WITH THE ONE AND ONLY STEPHEN HILLENBURG! 88
A SECRET REVEALED! 94
#1 SPONGEBOB FAN CERTIFICATE 97

Ahoy there!

Welcome to *The Insider's Guide to SpongeBob SquarePants*! You are going to learn the behind-the-scenes stories of how SpongeBob came to be, how the cartoons are made, and boatloads more!

Are you ready?

THE MAN Behind the NAUTICAL NONSENSE

The world was introduced to SpongeBob and his friends when the show was previewed on May 1, 1999, at the Twelfth Kids' Choice Awards. The show officially premiered July 17, 1999, on Nickelodeon. But how did SpongeBob spring to life in the first place? It all began with Stephen Hillenburg, SpongeBob's creator. If it wasn't for him, . . . well, let's not even think about that!

Stan Laurel

Jacques Cousteau

Oliver Hardy

Steve grew up in Anaheim, California. As a kid, his favorite things to do were diving, snorkeling, and drawing. He enjoyed watching old-time comedy movies featuring Stan Laurel and Oliver Hardy. He also loved to watch TV specials about Jacques Cousteau, the great French underwater explorer. Steve graduated from Humboldt State College in California. He taught marine science to kids at the Orange County

Marine Institute at Dana Point in Southern California (now called the Ocean Institute). It was there that he drew a comic book about all of the creatures that live in tide pools. Some of his drawings even looked like future SpongeBob characters!

After three years of teaching, Steve decided that what he really wanted to do for a living was draw. He went back to school for a master's degree in experimental animation at the California Institute of the Arts, which was founded by Walt Disney. His first animation job was on a Nickelodeon cartoon called *Rocko's Modern Life*. Soon Steve became the creative director of *Rocko's*, overseeing all the work that everyone did on the show. He worked with the writers, artists, and actors to make sure the show was the best it could be. Steve created one episode featuring a section about crazy underwater sea creatures. One day Steve showed his old tide pool comic book to writer Martin Olsen, and he said, "Are you crazy? This is your show."

Soon Steve found himself doodling sea sponge cartoon characters. He drew a character in the shape of a sponge and thought it was very funny. Something just felt right about it to him. Steve decided to create a show about all of the bizarre animals from under the sea. He thought a sea sponge would be the perfect hero! His idea for the main character was a man-child, an innocent undersea nerd. It was the perfect combination—a project that connected his knowledge of marine biology with his love of animation and art!

Steve worked with fellow artists Derek Drymon and Nick Jennings to develop the show idea. When they were ready, they presented the idea for SpongeBob to Nickelodeon. They brought along an aquarium, models of the characters, and lots of drawings. Steve also played the ukulele, did voices, made sound effects, and sang! He wore a Hawaiian shirt and put a tape recorder inside a conch shell that played the SpongeBob theme song. He wanted to make sure that Nickelodeon jumped out of their seats with excitement. The Nickelodeon executives loved the presentation. They were so exhausted from laughing, they had to take a moment to recover. When they finally stopped, Nickelodeon knew they had a special show in their hands. That day Nickelodeon said "Yes!" to SpongeBob.

Without further ado, let's meet the characters and talented cast who bring Bikini Bottom to life!

MEET THE CAST!

SPONGEBOB SquarePants

Likes: Jellyfishing, blowing bubbles, singing, karate, telling jokes, spreading cheer to his fellow Bikini Bottom inhabitants, and working at the Krusty Krab!

Dislikes: Stinky things and scary things!

Occupation: Fry-cook par excellence at the Krusty Krab restaurant.

Pet: A snail named Gary.

Best Friends: Patrick Star, Sandy Cheeks, and Squidward Tentacles.

Home: He lives in a two-story pineapple under the sea.

Favorite Hangouts: The Krusty Krab, Jellyfish Fields, and Goo Lagoon.

Usually Wears: White short-sleeve shirt, a tie, short brown pants, athletic socks, black shoes, and white underwear briefs.

Signature Quote: "I'm ready!"

Random Quote: "You taught me a valuable lesson, although I'm not quite sure what it was."

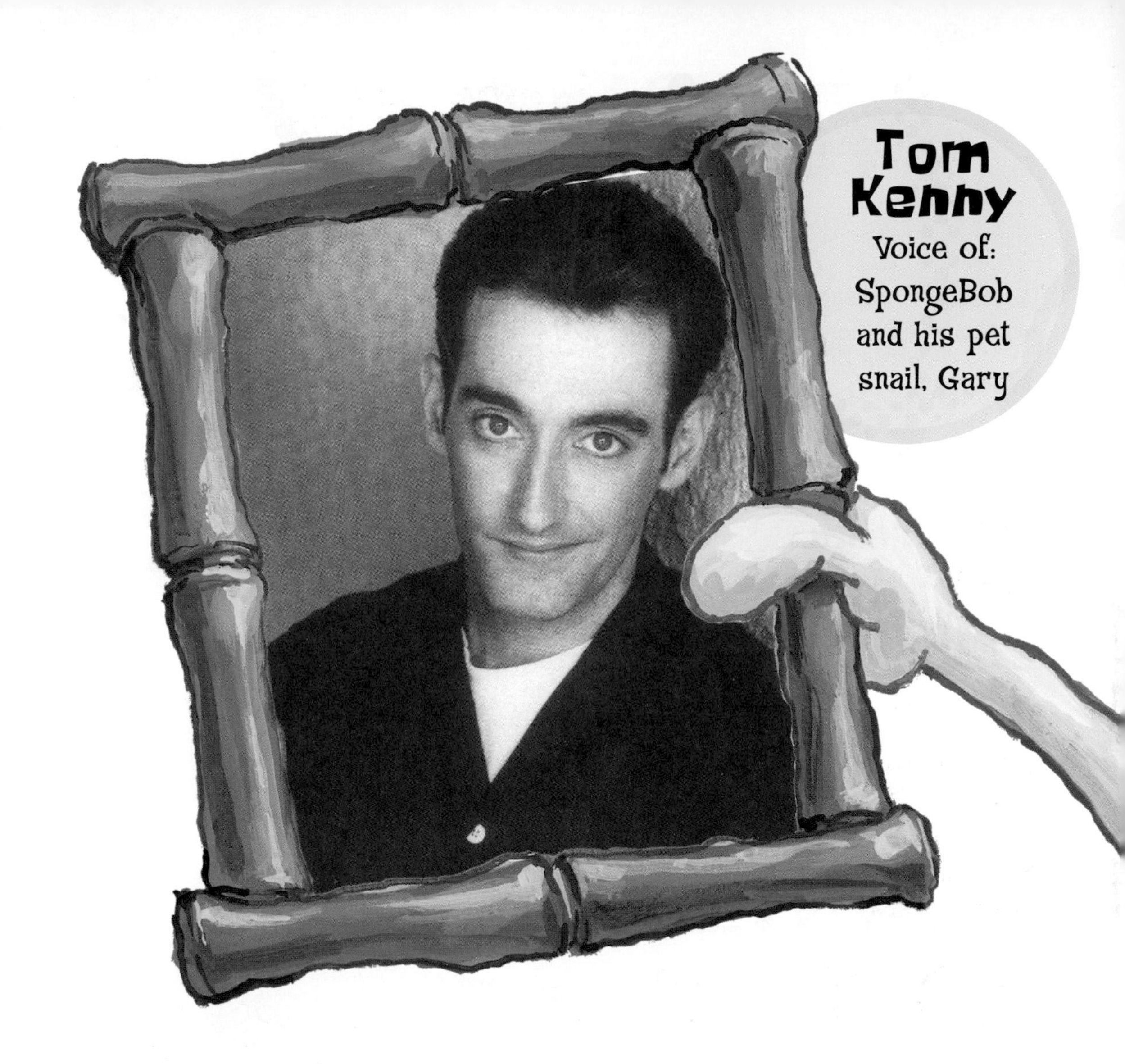

Tom's Take: Tom says SpongeBob's voice is a combination of the mayor of Munchkinland from *The Wizard of Oz* and Elroy Jetson from *The Jetsons!*

Other Cartoon Voices: Dog on *CatDog*, Heffer on *Rocko's Modern Life*, and the narrator on *The Powerpuff Girls*.

Nifty Fact: He also plays Patchy the Pirate.

Tom's Tips on How to Laugh Like SpongeBob: Make a "ba-a-a-a" sound like a dolphin or sheep, and very, very gently move your hand up and down your Adam's apple really fast!

PATRICK Star

Likes: Sleeping, eating anything, and doing whatever SpongeBob is doing.

Dislikes: Not sleeping and not eating.

Occupation: Napping, snoozing, and dozing.

Weird Habit: Wakes up at three A.M. to eat Krabby Patties.

Best Friend: SpongeBob.

Home: He lives underneath a rock.

Favorite Hangout: Any comfortable place to rest.

Usually Wears: Green bathing shorts with purple flowers on them.

Signature Quote: "Zzzzzzzzzzzz . . ."

Random Quote: "That is the stench of discovery."

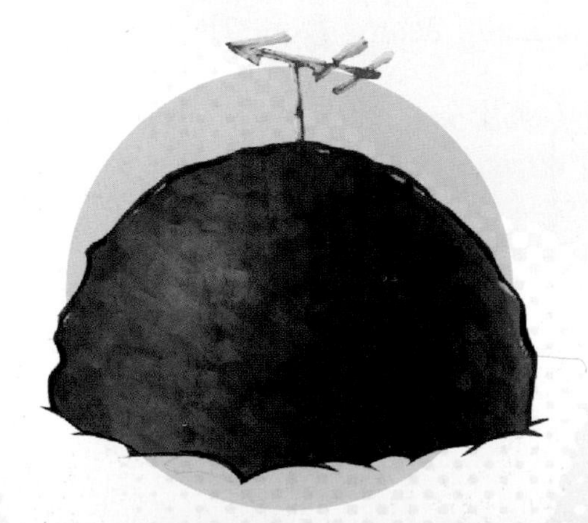

Other Cartoon Voices and Showbiz Stuff: He's also done cartoon voices for *Gargoyles* and *Jumanji*. He played the part of Michael "Dauber" Dybinski on the TV show *Coach* and has appeared on *Sabrina, the Teenage Witch*.

Nifty Fact: Bill is six feet six inches tall!

SQUIDWARD Tentacles

Likes: Peace and quiet, playing the clarinet (which he nicknamed "Clary"), painting pictures of himself, and soaking in a nice hot tub.

Dislikes: SpongeBob and Patrick, but mostly SpongeBob.

Occupation: Cashier at the Krusty Krab.

Nemesis: Squilliam Fancyson, his high school rival who is very successful in everything that Squidward wishes he could be. Squilliam never misses an opportunity to show off his talents and fortune.

Home: A tiki head with an uninviting expression.

Favorite Hangout: His warm bathtub or anywhere far away from SpongeBob.

Usually Wears: A short-sleeve collared shirt. No pants.

Signature Quote: "How did I ever get surrounded by such loser neighbors?!"

Random Quote: "Stay back, I've got garden tools."

Other Cartoon Voices: Jorgen Von Strangle on *The Fairly OddParents*, and Professor Membrane in *Invader ZIM*. He has also done voices in such movies as *Toy Story 2*; *Monsters, Inc.*; *Lilo & Stitch*; and *Treasure Planet*.

Nifty Fact: He has a fear of sharks and giant squids.

Rodger Bumpass

Voice of: Squidward Tentacles

MR. Eugene H. KRABS

Likes: Money and his daughter, Pearl (in that order).

Dislikes: Losing a penny.

Occupation: Owner and founder of the Krusty Krab. He has also been a sailor, a pirate, and owner of the Rusty Krab retirement home (which he turned into the Krusty Krab).

Best Friend: Money.

Home: A black anchor.

Favorite Hangout: As close to his money as possible.

Usually Wears: Short-sleeve shirt, blue pants, and a big, black belt.

Signature Quote: "Arrggh!"

Random Quote: "It sounds like . . . the pitter-patter of . . . MONEY!!"

Clancy Brown

Voice of: Mr. Krabs

Other Cartoon Voices and Showbiz Stuff: Clancy has also done voices for other cartoons like *Star Wars: Bounty Hunter*, *Crash Bandicoot*, *Jackie Chan Adventures*, *Mighty Ducks the Movie*, and *Superman*! As an actor, he was in *Starship Troopers*, *The Adventures of Buckaroo Banzai Across the Eighth Dimension*, the "bad guy" from *Highlander*, HBO's *Carnivàle*, and the TV show *ER*.

Nifty Fact: Clancy collects animation art.

SANDY *Cheeks*

Likes: Texas, karate, surfing, skiing, yodeling, weight lifting, and extreme sports.

Dislikes: Water in her helmet.

Occupation: Adventurer!

Pets: Wormy (a caterpillar who turned into a butterfly), a cricket, Snaky the Snake, and birds.

Best Friend: SpongeBob.

Home: An underwater treedome filled with air.

Favorite Hangout: Mussel Beach.

Usually Wears: Space suit, and a helmet with a flower on it.

Signature Quote: "Don't you dare take the name of Texas in vain!"

Random Quote: "Don't you have to be stupid somewhere else?"

Carolyn Lawrence

Voice of:
Everybody's favorite squirrel, Sandy Cheeks

Other Cartoon Voices and Showbiz Stuff: Carolyn was the voice of Cindy Vortex in the movie *Jimmy Neutron: Boy Genius* and in the TV series *The Adventures of Jimmy Neutron, Boy Genius*. You also may have seen her on the TV show *7th Heaven*.

Nifty Fact: She's not from Texas!

Sheldon PLANKTON

Likes: Being evil.

Dislikes: Not having the secret recipe to Krabby Patties!

Occupation: Owner of the Chum Bucket, the world's worst fast-food restaurant, where the menu includes Living Hand Burgers and Chumbalaya.

Pets: None. Who would want to be his pet?

Best Friend: Karen (his computer wife), or anyone who will give him the secret recipe to Krabby Patties!

Pretend Best Friend: SpongeBob. Plankton once befriended SpongeBob in an attempt to get the Krabby Patty recipe.

Home: The Chum Bucket. He lives where he works.

Favorite Hangout: The Krusty Krab (for spying purposes).

Usually Wears: A mean one-eyed expression.

Signature Quote: "You blasted barnacle head!"

Random Quote: "Victory, thy name is Plankton."

LARRY the Lobster

Likes: To get tan, lift weights, and whiten his teeth.

Dislikes: To be pale and wimpy.

Occupation: Sometimes lifeguards at Goo Lagoon.

Favorite Hangout: Spends most of his time working out at Mussel Beach.

Signature Quote: "You guys wanna go lift some weights?"

Random Quote: "Dude, you're ripped!!!"

Mr. Lawrence

Voice of: Plankton, Larry the Lobster, and many of the random fish on the show. He is also a writer and an artist.

Other Cartoon Voices: Filburt Shellbach in *Rocko's Modern Life.*

Nifty Fact: His first name, which he rarely uses, is Doug.

GARY

Likes: Sleeping and being with SpongeBob, his owner.

Dislikes: Baths.

Occupation: Pet.

Pets: None. He is a pet.

Home: SpongeBob's house.

Usually Wears: A shell.

Signature Quote: "Meow."

Random Quote: "Meow."

Tom Kenny does Gary's voice.

"MEEEEOW."

Directions For Feeding Gary

If you ever find yourself snail-sitting Gary, or any other snail, follow these three simple instructions for a happy, healthy snail.

1. Locate snail food.

2. Find empty snail bowl.

3. Fill empty snail bowl.

PEARL Krabs

Likes: Being a pretty and popular teenage whale and hanging out with other pretty and popular teenagers.

Dislikes: Being embarrassed by her thrifty father; wearing out-of-date fashions.

Occupation: Student and cheerleader.

Pets: None.

Home: Lives with her father, Mr. Krabs, in a black anchor.

Usually Wears: Something very trendy.

Signature Quote: "You really shouldn't have!"

Random Quote: "This job is cutting majorly into my social life."

Pearl

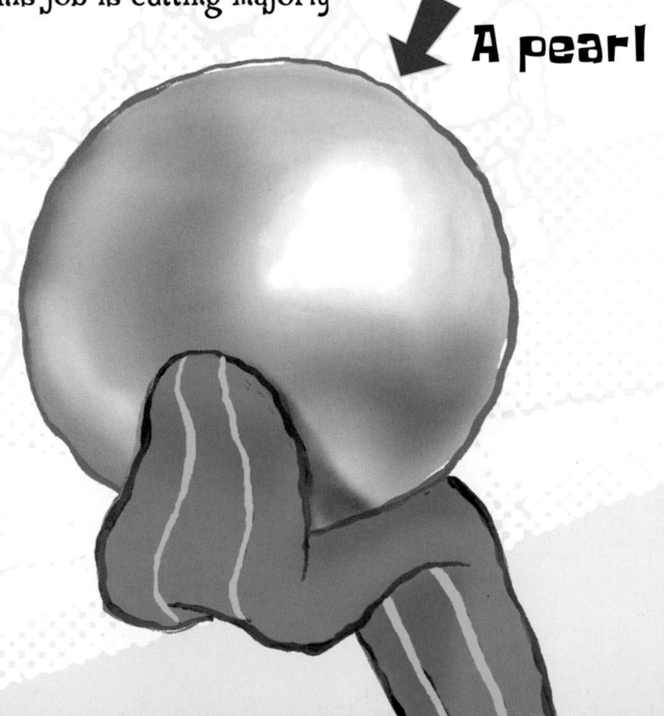

A pearl

Lori Alan does Pearl's voice.

MRS. PUFF

Likes: Teaching.

Dislikes: Teaching SpongeBob; blowing up (she's a puffer fish).

Occupation: Bikini Bottom Boating School Instructor.

Pets: None.

Husband: None; he was caught by a fisherman and turned into a lamp. Mrs. Puff did go on a date with Mr. Krabs once.

Home: Pink house.

Usually Wears: Hat, tasteful blouse, and skirt.

Signature Quote: "Oh, SpongeBob."

Random Quote: "I'll have to move to a new city, start a new boating school with a new name! No, not again!"

Mary Jo Catlett does the voice of Mrs. Puff.

MERMAIDMAN

Likes: Napping, eating soft food, and fighting evil.

Dislikes: Man Ray and the Dirty Bubble.

Occupation: Retired superhero.

Pets: None.

Home: Shady Shoals Rest Home.

Usually Wears: Green tights, green gloves, pink slippers, and a starfish mask.

Signature Quote: "By the power of Neptune!"

Random Quote: "EVIL!" or "To the meatloaf!"

Mermaidman's voice is done by Ernest Borgnine. Borgnine won the Academy Award for Best Actor in 1955 for the movie *Marty*.

BARNACLEBOY

Likes: Napping, eating soft food, and fighting evil.

Dislikes: Being treated like a kid.

Occupation: Mermaidman's faithful sidekick (retired).

Pets: None.

Home: Shady Shoals Rest Home.

Usually Wears: A sailor hat, mask, and cape.

Signature Quote: "Will you stop calling me 'boy'!"

Random Quote: "Where did we park the invisible boatmobile?"

Barnacleboy's voice is done by Tim Conway, who won an Emmy Award for *The Carol Burnett Show*.

Mermaidman and Barnacleboy—preretirement . . .

DID YOU KNOW?

Waterlogged Trivia

SpongeBob's character was influenced by Jerry Lewis, Pee Wee Herman, and Charlie Chaplin.

While looking at a picture of SpongeBob, Tom Kenny said, "Boy, look at this sponge in square pants, thinking he can get a job in a fast-food place." Steve Hillenburg thought the phrase "square pants" was hilarious, so it became SpongeBob's last name!

Squidward is an octopus, NOT a squid!

In 1996 Steve Hillenburg did the original voice of Squidward on an early audio test with Tom Kenny as SpongeBob.

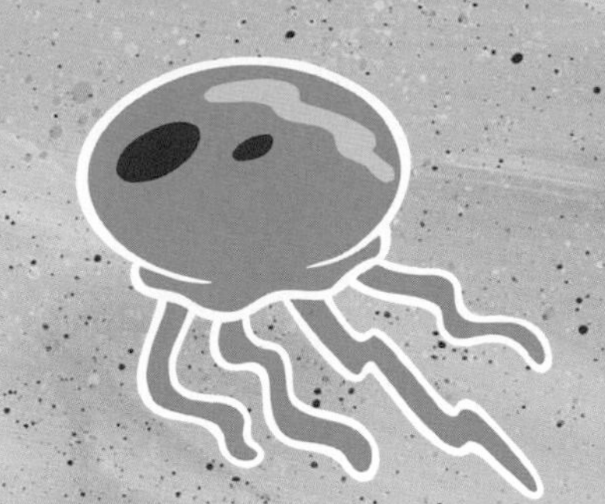

SpongeBob was originally called Sponge Boy. But the name had already been trademarked, so Steve couldn't use it.

Steve Hillenburg thought of the name Bikini Bottom while driving in his car.

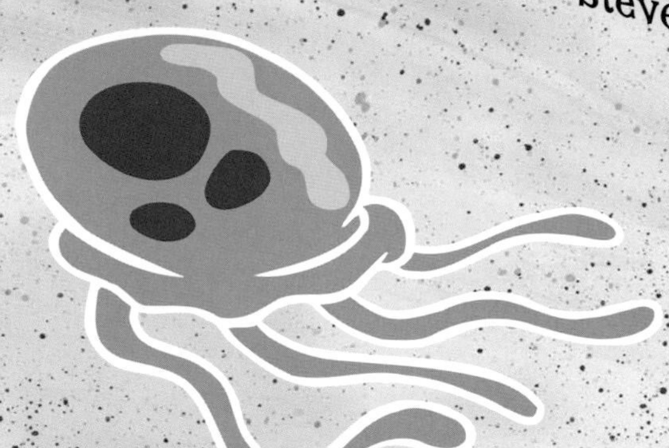

The Krusty Krab was originally named the "Crusty Crab," but it looked funnier to spell it incorrectly!

When Steve Hillenburg first drew SpongeBob, he looked like a real sea sponge (like SpongeBob's parents). He decided it'd be funnier to have him resemble a kitchen sponge!

Those are none other than Steve Hillenburg's lips, as Patchy the Pirate, singing the SpongeBob theme song.

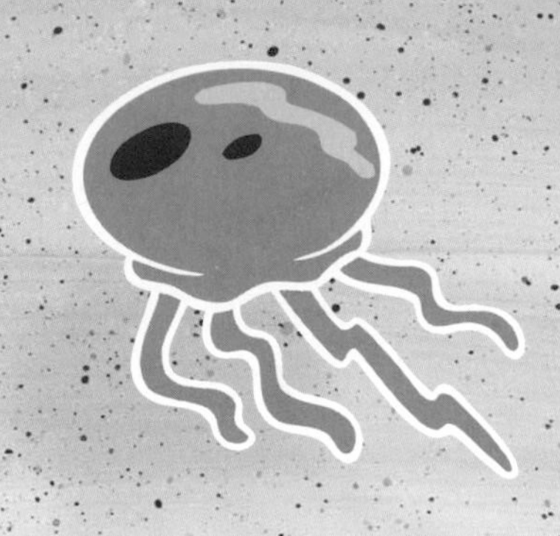

The song heard in the SpongeBob pilot, "Living in the Sunlight, Loving in the Moonlight," was written more than seventy-four years ago!

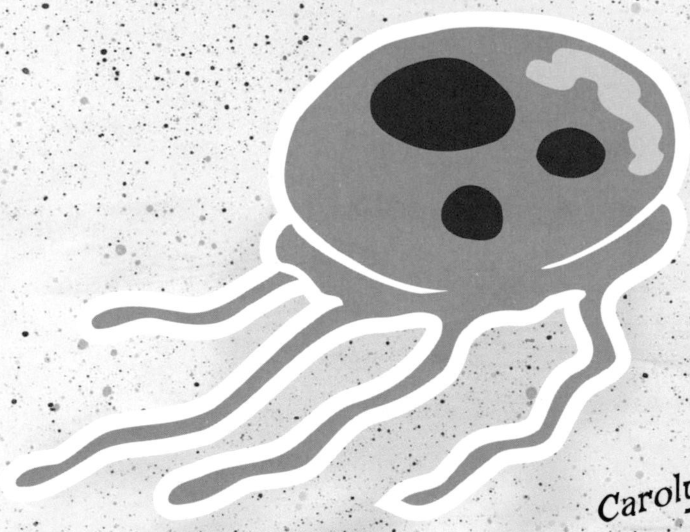

Carolyn Lawrence fashioned the voice of Sandy Cheeks after Academy Award–winning actress Holly Hunter.

When Bill Fagerbakke does the voice of Patrick getting mad, he thinks of Academy Award-winning actress Shelly Winters.

The voice of Karen, Plankton's computer wife, is done by Tom Kenny's wife, actress Jill Talley.

Steve Hillenburg plays the ukulele and surfs.

Barnacleboy was originally named Barnacle Bill and had a log body. His face looked like Popeye, and he had a pipe hanging from his mouth!

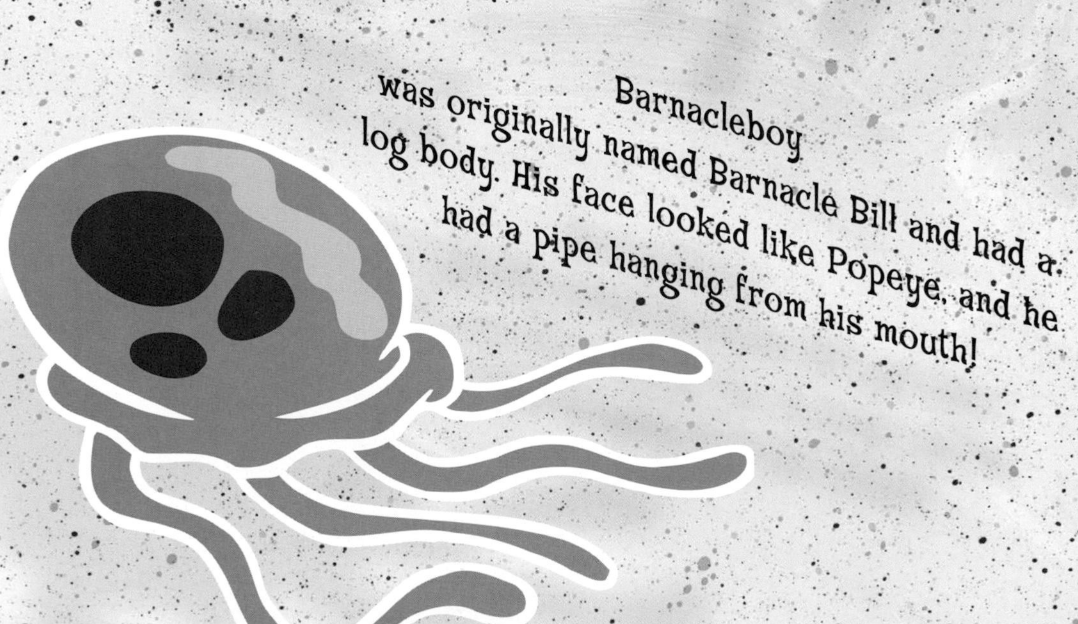

HOME SWEET HOMES!

Check out some of the things found inside and outside the homes of some of Bikini Bottom's leading citizens.

SPONGEBOB'S PINEAPPLE-SHAPED HOUSE

Well-appointed library!

Cozy bedroom with foghorn alarm clock!
GARY
Deluxe bathroom!
Spacious kitchen!

SQUIDWARD'S HOUSE

Shaped like the famous Easter Island statues, this home was built out of volcanic rock.

There are strange things in Squidward's closet. . . .

Rooftop sunbathing!

SANDY'S TREEDOME

Picnic table!
Special air-lock entrance to admit undersea friends!

TV antennae on roof.
Basically a hole in the ground.

WHO SAID WHAT?

Here are some quotes from SpongeBob SquarePants. Do you know who said them?

1. "I smell the smelly smell of something that smells smelly!"
2. "My ice cream! It's alive!"
3. "Remember: Licking doorknobs is illegal on other planets."
4. "That's it, mister! You just lost your brain privileges!"
5. "Every day is a holiday for SpongeBob, even if he has to make one up."
6. "Now let's play a classic. Find the hay in the needle stack!"
7. "Look! It's SpongeBob NudiePants!"
8. "That's it, I'm getting off the loony express!"

1)Mr. Krabs; 2)Patrick; 3)SpongeBob; 4)Plankton; 5)Narrator; 6)Sandy; 7)Pearl; 8)Squidward

Will the Real SpongeBob PLEASE STAND UP?

Here are some facts about real sea sponges—not to be confused with facts about the real SpongeBob!

There are more than five thousand different kinds of sea sponges! (There is only one SpongeBob SquarePants.)

People use sea sponges for cleaning and bathing. (SpongeBob loves the bath!)

Sea sponges live under the water, attached to rocks, plants, and other objects, though some are free floating (like SpongeBob).

Sponges are among the oldest kinds of animals. Fossils have been found of marine sponges that lived more than five hundred million years ago. (SpongeBob has some ancient relatives!)

Some sea sponges are bigger than people! (Imagine a seven-foot-tall SpongeBob!)

Modern science is investigating some of the things found inside sea sponges, which could one day cure a host of human diseases. (Will a sponge a day keep the doctor away?)

Sea sponges don't have heads, arms, or internal organs (or square pants).

SPONGEBOB'S Come a Long Way, Baby!

SpongeBob didn't always look the way he does today. Check out these original drawings from the depths of the SpongeBob historical files.

Here is an early piece of artwork showing the characters in different vehicles. In these drawings Steve Hillenburg was creating the visual style of the show.

A very early concept of Squidward and SpongeBob. Many different versions of the characters are drawn before a final decision is made.

An early concept of Patrick and the buildings of Bikini Bottom. Notice that the Krusty Krab is called "Capt. Crabs." Simple, rough sketches are created to show how characters will look from different angles, and their spatial relationship to buildings and objects.

SPONGEBOY
ESSENCE DE SPONGE
NAKED!
'CRUSTY' UNIFORM
PLUS SAFETY GLASSES!

Even in the early days SpongeBob was a master bubble blower!

Some SpongeBob expressions!

Mr. Krabs has always been hungry for money!

Sandy was Texas-tough, even in the beginning!

An early map of Bikini Bottom resembles much of what is seen in the show today.

On January 20, 1997, he was still called Sponge Boy!

SPONGE BOY

PATRICK

1 · 20 · 97

BEHIND THE SCENES
The Making of SpongeBob SquarePants

You may not realize it, but creating one episode of *SpongeBob SquarePants* takes a lot of people doing a lot of hard work!

Each new episode starts with a story idea. Steve Hillenburg and the writers create a story outline of about two pages. The outline explains what will happen in the beginning, middle, and end of the episode.

Next come the storyboard artists. A storyboard is kind of like a comic strip, with three sketches on a page, drawn in pencil. The storyboard artists decide what the characters will say and do. The characters' speeches are called the "dialogue."

Next the artists write the dialogue below each corresponding sketch. The storyboard artists usually work in teams of two people. It takes about three hundred drawings to finish just one storyboard. The storyboard gives everyone an idea of what the actual cartoon episode will look like.

The artists then present the storyboard to Steve Hillenburg and the creative director, Derek Drymon. This presentation is called a "pitch." They pin the pages on a wall, then act out the scenes. They talk about what works and what doesn't work. Then the artists go back to the drawing board, and make changes as a result of their pitch. They pitch the storyboard again to Steve and Derek, and finally to the entire *SpongeBob* crew!

When everyone agrees on and is happy with the storyboard, another group of artists, called the "storyboard finishers," redraw the entire storyboard to show exactly what the characters and backgrounds will look like. These drawings are more detailed and cleaner than the sketches.

The actors go into a recording studio at Nickelodeon Animation Studios, in Burbank, California, to record the script. There are two recording engineers who make sure that the voices are recorded clearly. A script supervisor keeps track of all the "takes." Takes are the best versions of the lines the directors choose. Sometimes the actors, especially Tom Kenny, make up lines on the spot to make the episode even funnier! Many times the actors crack one another up, and they have to rerecord a line because they are laughing so much! If there is a song, like "The F.U.N. Song" or "Texas," they will record that, too.

Next, the storyboard and the tape of the voices are put together in an "animatic." They film the storyboard pictures with a video camera and add the recorded voices. This way they can look at the videotape, see the drawings, and hear the voices all at the same time. It's like looking at a comic book but hearing the words read out loud. There is no movement or animation yet. The animatic includes the voices so the producers and directors can decide if a story seems too long or too short.

Background artists then draw the backgrounds—colorful, detailed paintings of Bikini Bottom's environment. In most cartoons the backgrounds stay the same, but in *SpongeBob SquarePants*, the rooms in his house or in the Krusty Krab can change a lot! Real photographs are also used for the talking fish newscaster, the water above Bikini Bottom, and pictures of real sea sponges and starfish.

The finished storyboards and backgrounds are sent to Rough Draft Studios in Seoul, South Korea, where the animation is completed. Artists draw the characters on clear plastic sheets, called "cels," so the backgrounds can show through. Each movement of the character is on one cel. It takes more than ten thousand cels to make *one* SpongeBob cartoon!

The cels are placed on top of the backgrounds and photographed by a special animation movie camera–one cel at a time! When the film is developed, it is sent back to Nickelodeon Studios in Burbank.

At Nickelodeon Studios the picture editor combines the film animation with the audiotape of the voices. If a scene is too long, he or she will edit it to make it shorter. Next, the sound editor adds sound effects, like a phone ringing or a door slamming, to match the actions.

The music editor watches the tape and comes up with music for the episode. Most of the time, preexisting music or songs are used on *SpongeBob*, like "Living in the Sunlight, Loving in the Moonlight."

Finally, after about nine months of work, a *SpongeBob* cartoon is finished!

So . . . You Call Yourself a Fan?

Do you think you've seen every episode of *SpongeBob SquarePants* so far? Check out the episode guide below and see if you've missed any.

1A) "HELP WANTED"
Premiere Date: 5/1/99
SpongeBob gets a job at the Krusty Krab and battles angry anchovies!

1A EXTENSION) "REEF BLOWERS"
Premiere Date: 5/1/99
SpongeBob uses a reef blower to clean up his yard . . . much to Squidward's dismay.

1B) "TEA AT THE TREEDOME"
Premiere Date: 5/1/99
SpongeBob meets Sandy Cheeks for the first time and is introduced to air. He struggles to impress his new friend in her waterless treedome but soon discovers the perils of life without water.

2A) "BUBBLESTAND"
Premiere Date: 7/17/99
SpongeBob opens a bubblestand, and teaches Squidward the art of bubble blowing. Squidward's plan to humiliate SpongeBob "blows up" in his face.

2B) "RIPPED PANTS"
Premiere Date: 7/17/99
SpongeBob rips his pants at the beach, and everyone finds it hilarious . . . until SpongeBob takes the joke too far.

3A) "JELLYFISHING"
Premiere Date: 7/31/99
While Squidward is recovering from a bicycling accident, SpongeBob and Patrick take him out jellyfishing, so he can have his "best day ever." *Not.*

3B) "PLANKTON!"
Premiere Date: 7/31/99
Plankton tries to steal the secret Krabby Patty formula by using a mind-control device on SpongeBob!

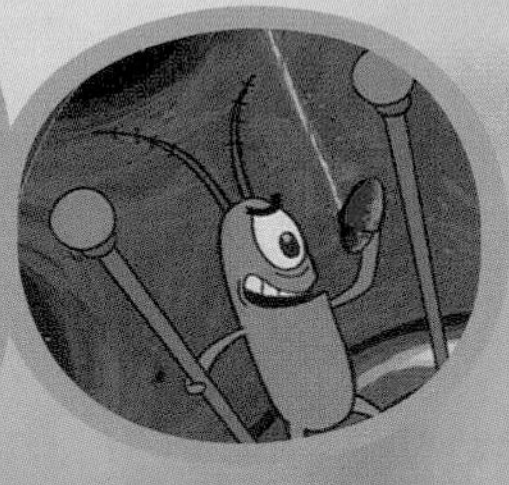

4A) "NAUGHTY NAUTICAL NEIGHBORS"
Premiere Date: 8/7/99
Squidward tricks SpongeBob and Patrick into not being friends so he can have some peace and quiet. But the plan backfires on Squidward.

4B) "BOATING SCHOOL"
Premiere Date: 8/7/99
SpongeBob takes his boating driving test, and Patrick tries to help. All goes well until SpongeBob realizes he might be cheating.

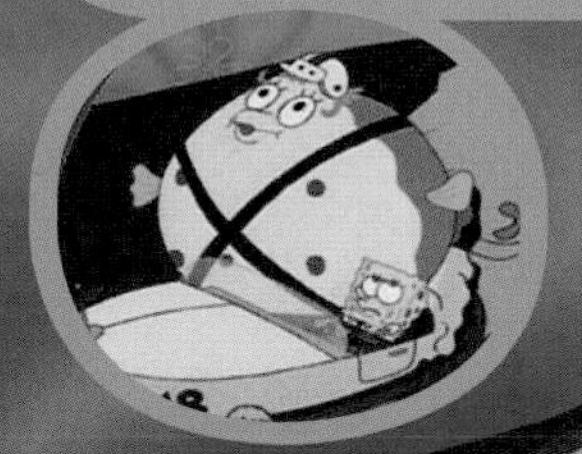

5A) "PIZZA DELIVERY"
Premiere Date: 8/14/99
Squidward and SpongeBob get stranded in the middle of nowhere while trying to deliver a Krabby Patty pizza.

5B) "HOME SWEET PINEAPPLE"
Premiere Date: 8/14/99
Nematodes destroy SpongeBob's house, and he tries to move back in with his parents.

6A) "MERMAID MAN AND BARNACLE BOY"
Premiere Date: 8/21/99
SpongeBob and Patrick try to convince their favorite superhero team, Mermaidman and Barnacleboy, to come out of retirement.

6B) "PICKLES"
Premiere Date: 8/21/99
SpongeBob gives up making Krabby Patties when he once forgets to put in pickles.

7A) "HALL MONITOR"
Premiere Date: 8/28/99
SpongeBob gets carried away when appointed hall monitor at Mrs. Puff's boating school. Taking the law into his own hands, SpongeBob wreaks havoc on all who cross his path.

7B) "JELLYFISH JAM"
Premiere Date: 8/28/99
SpongeBob keeps a jellyfish as a pet until it brings its fellow jellyfish to the ultimate party!

8A) "SANDY'S ROCKET"

Premiere Date: 9/17/99
SpongeBob and Patrick accidentally set off Sandy's rocket and go into space! . . . So they think.

8B) "SQUEAKY BOOTS"

Premiere Date: 9/17/99
Mr. Krabs gives SpongeBob a pair of squeaky boots instead of a paycheck. Krabs' conscience haunts him as the squeaking noise drives him crazy.

9A) "NATURE PANTS"

Premiere Date: 9/11/99
SpongeBob quits his job and gives up his possessions to rough it in JellyFish Fields with the jellyfish.

9B) "OPPOSITE DAY"

Premiere Date: 9/11/99
Squidward decides to sell his house. He fools SpongeBob and Patrick into thinking that it's Opposite Day, so potential buyers won't know how annoying they really are.

10A) "CULTURE SHOCK"

Premiere Date: 9/18/99
Squidward runs a talent show at the Krusty Krab but doesn't let SpongeBob take part.

10B) "F.U.N."

Premiere Date: 9/18/99
SpongeBob starts to feel sorry for Plankton, so he invites him out for a day of fun.

11A) "MUSCLEBOB BUFFPANTS"

Premiere Date: 10/2/99
SpongeBob orders fake muscles and enters the annual Mussel Beach Anchor Toss competition.

11B) "SQUIDWARD, THE UNFRIENDLY GHOST"
Premiere Date: 10/2/99
SpongeBob and Patrick think they've killed Squidward and that he's a ghost!

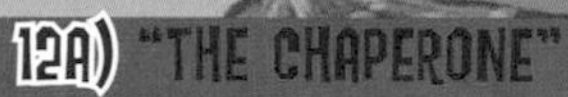

12A) "THE CHAPERONE"
Premiere Date: 3/8/00
Pearl's prom date stands her up, and SpongeBob agrees to fill in.

12B) "EMPLOYEE OF THE MONTH"
Premiere Date: 3/8/00
SpongeBob and Squidward compete for the Employee of the Month award.

13A) "SCAREDY PANTS"
Premiere Date: 10/28/99
SpongeBob tries to scare everyone in his Flying Dutchman costume at the Krusty Krab Halloween party.

13B) "I WAS A TEENAGE GARY"
Premiere Date: 10/28/99
Gary becomes ill after Squidward neglects him while snail-sitting for SpongeBob. SpongeBob accidentally takes Gary's medicine and turns into SpongeSnail.

14A) "SB-129"
Premiere Date: 12/31/99
After being trapped in a freezer for years, and thawed out, Squidward finds himself two thousand years ahead in a futuristic Bikini Bottom.

14B) "KARATE CHOPPERS"
Premiere Date: 12/31/99
Mr. Krabs tells SpongeBob to stop doing karate with Sandy, or he'll be fired!

15A) "SLEEPY TIME"
Premiere Date: 1/17/00
SpongeBob's dream-self enters the dreams of others. . . . And they don't like it one bit!

15B) "SUDS"
Premiere Date: 1/17/00
SpongeBob gets sick with the suds but is afraid to go to the doctor.

16A) "VALENTINE'S DAY"
Premiere Date: 2/14/00
When SpongeBob has trouble delivering Patrick's special Valentine's Day gift, Patrick gets angry. Very angry.

16B) "THE PAPER"
Premiere Date: 2/14/00
SpongeBob has fun with a gum wrapper that Squidward discards, causing Squidward to feel envious that SpongeBob can have a blast with a worthless piece of paper.

17A)
"Arrgh!"
Premiere Date: 3/15/00
Mr. Krabs takes SpongeBob and Patrick on a treasure hunt using a map from a game.

17B) "ROCK BOTTOM"

Premiere Date: 3/15/00
SpongeBob misses the bus home from Glove World and can't get back!

18A) "TEXAS"

Premiere Date: 3/22/00
Sandy wants to return to Texas, so SpongeBob and Patrick try to bring Texas to her.

18B) "WALKING SMALL"

Premiere Date: 3/22/00
Plankton tries to trick SpongeBob into being more aggressive. SpongeBob realizes that it's more fun to be nice to people than to have them obey you because you're mean.

19A) "FOOLS IN APRIL"

Premiere Date: 4/1/00
It's April Fools' Day, SpongeBob's favorite holiday, and Squidward tries to pull the ultimate prank.

19B) "NEPTUNE'S SPATULA"

Premiere Date: 4/1/00
After SpongeBob pulls an ancient golden spatula from a vat of grease, Neptune appears and challenges SpongeBob to the Ultimate Cook-Off Challenge.

20A) "HOOKY"

Premiere Date: 3/3/01
Dangerous fishing hooks appear in Bikini Bottom, and SpongeBob and Patrick start riding them!

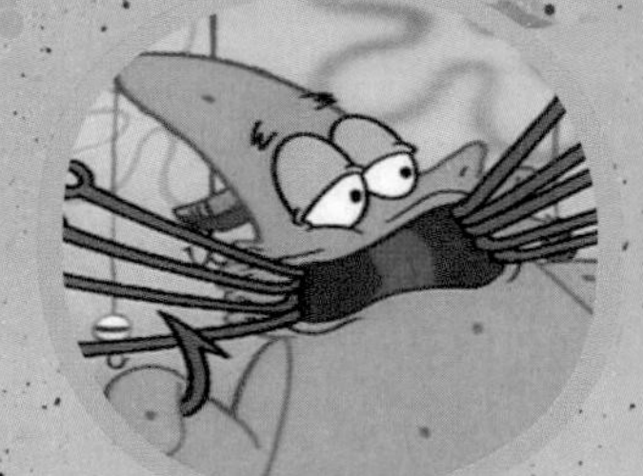

20B) "MERMAIDMAN AND BARNACLEBOY II"
Premiere Date: 3/3/01
SpongeBob wins the Conch Call, and calls Mermaidman and Barnacleboy whenever there's danger. . . . Or not.

21A) "YOUR SHOE'S UNTIED!"
Premiere Date: 2/17/01
SpongeBob tries to teach Patrick how to tie his shoes, but ends up forgetting how! Gary saves the day by teaching SpongeBob a lace-tying song to help him remember.

21B) "SQUID'S DAY OFF"
Premiere Date: 2/17/01
When Squidward's left in charge of the Krusty Krab, his first order of business is to turn everything over to SpongeBob and take the rest of the day off.

22A) "SOMETHING SMELLS"
Premiere Date: 10/20/00
When everyone avoids SpongeBob after he eats a sea-onion sundae, Patrick convinces SpongeBob he must be ugly.

22B) "BOSSY BOOTS"
Premiere Date: 10/20/00
Pearl turns the Krusty Krab into a hip, happening teenage hangout. But the Krusty Krab is losing money, so Mr. Krabs orders SpongeBob to fire her or lose his own job!

23A) "BIG PINK LOSER"
Premiere Date: 2/3/01
Patrick is sad because he can't win any awards, so SpongeBob suggests that he get a job at the Krusty Krab.

23B) "BUBBLE BUDDY"
Premiere Date: 2/3/01
SpongeBob creates his own friend out of bubbles, and ends up irritating everyone. They insist Bubble Buddy isn't real, until they discover just how wrong they are.

24A) "DYING FOR PIE"
Premiere Date: 1/27/01
Squidward buys an explosive pie from pirates, and he feels guilty because he thinks SpongeBob accidentally ate it.

24B) "IMITATION KRABS"
Premiere Date: 1/27/01
Plankton creates a robotic duplicate of Mr. Krabs to trick SpongeBob into giving him the Krabby Patty secret formula.

25A) "WORMY"
Premiere Date: 2/24/01
SpongeBob and Patrick pet-sit Sandy's worm, and they think it's a monster when it turns into a butterfly!

25B) "PATTY HYPE"
Premiere Date: 2/24/01
Mr. Krabs laughs at SpongeBob's idea for Pretty Patties, so SpongeBob opens his own stand in front of his house.

26A) "GRANDMA'S KISSES"
Premiere Date: 4/28/01
SpongeBob gets made fun of after being kissed by his grandma, so he decides to act more like an adult, which means no more kisses from grandma.

26B) "SQUIDVILLE"
Premiere Date: 4/28/01
Squidward moves to Tentacle Acres, a private town where only octopi live, but quickly gets bored.

27A) "PRE-HIBERNATION WEEK"
Premiere Date: 5/5/01
Sandy is on a mission to live it up before hibernating, but her games are too dangerous for SpongeBob, and he goes into hiding.

27B) "LIFE OF CRIME"
Premiere Date: 5/5/01
SpongeBob and Patrick "borrow" a balloon, but after it pops, they go on the lam.

28 A/B) "CHRISTMAS WHO?"
Premiere Date: 12/7/00
SpongeBob tries to bring Christmas to Bikini Bottom, but Santa never comes. Everyone is disappointed and angry, and the person who was most against Christmas ends up saving it for all of Bikini Bottom.

29A) "SURVIVAL OF THE IDIOTS"
Premiere Date: 5/19/01
SpongeBob and Patrick disrupt Sandy's winter hibernation and she enters a terrifying sleepwalking, sleep-talking haze.

29B) "DUMPED"
Premiere Date: 5/19/01
Much to SpongeBob's dismay, Gary starts following Patrick around. SpongeBob becomes desperate to win back Gary's love.

30A) "NO FREE RIDES"
Premiere Date: 4/14/01
Mrs. Puff is tired of SpongeBob in her class so she passes him, but then steals his boat to prevent him from hurting someone.

30B) "I'M YOUR BIGGEST FANATIC"
Premiere Date: 4/14/01
SpongeBob goes jellyfishing with members of an elite jellyfishing club.

31A) "MERMAID MAN AND BARNACLEBOY III"
Premiere Date: 9/14/01
Mermaidman and Barnacleboy go on vacation, leaving SpongeBob and Patrick to take care of the Mermalair. A showdown ensues with Man Ray, a not-so-evil villain.

31B) "SQUIRREL JOKES"
Premiere Date: 9/14/01
SpongeBob tells mean squirrel jokes when he performs stand-up at the Krusty Krab. Sandy is offended and asks SpongeBob to stop.

32A) "PRESSURE"
Premiere Date: 5/12/01
A fierce battle erupts when SpongeBob and Sandy argue over whether sea creatures or land creatures are better at sports.

33A) "SHANGHAIED"
Premiere Date: 7/26/03
The Flying Dutchman makes SpongeBob, Patrick, and Squidward his ghostly crew.

32B) "THE SMOKING PEANUT"
Premiere Date: 5/12/01
SpongeBob makes the famous Clamu oyster cry, resulting in the anger of everyone in Bikini Bottom.

33B) "GARY TAKES A BATH"
Premiere Date: 7/26/03
Gary uses his smarts to outwit SpongeBob in order to avoid taking a bath.

34A) "WELCOME TO THE CHUM BUCKET"
Premiere Date: 1/21/01
Mr. Krabs loses SpongeBob's fry cook contract to Plankton in a card game.

34B) "FRANKENDOODLE"
Premiere Date: 1/21/01
SpongeBob and Patrick find a magic pencil that makes drawings come to life.

35A) "THE SECRET BOX"
Premiere Date: 9/7/01
Patrick shows his secret box to SpongeBob, but won't show him what's inside.

35B) "BAND GEEKS"
Premiere Date: 9/7/01
Squidward rushes to assemble a marching band for the Bubble Bowl so he can one-up his high school rival, Squilliam.

36A) "THE GRAVEYARD SHIFT"
Premiere Date: 9/6/02
Squidward scares SpongeBob with his story about the Hash-slinging Slasher!

36B) "KRUSTY LOVE"
Premiere Date: 9/6/02
To show how much he likes her, Mr. Krabs spends tons of money on a first date with Mrs. Puff.

37A) "PROCRASTINATION"
Premiere Date: 10/19/01
SpongeBob doesn't want to write an essay for boating school, so he comes up with a bunch of excuses not to.

37B) "I'M WITH STUPID"
Premiere Date: 10/19/01
Patrick's parents visit, and SpongeBob agrees to act incredibly stupid to make Patrick seem smart.

38A) "SAILOR MOUTH"
Premiere Date: 9/21/01
SpongeBob and Patrick learn a "bad" word, and Mr. Krabs warns them never to use it again.

38B) "ARTIST UNKNOWN"
Premiere Date: 9/21/01
SpongeBob takes Squidward's art class, and Squidward is jealous to learn SpongeBob is the better artist.

39B) "THE FRY COOK GAMES"
Premiere Date: 9/28/01
At the annual Fry Cook games, SpongeBob and Patrick compete against each other.

39A) "JELLYFISH HUNTER"
Premiere Date: 9/28/01
When people fall in love with SpongeBob's Krabby Patties with jellyfish jelly, Mr. Krabs gets SpongeBob to capture almost every jellyfish in Jellyfish Fields to make more.

40A) "SQUID ON STRIKE"
Premiere Date: 10/12/01
Squidward is fed up with the unfairness at the Krusty Krab, and decides to go on strike.

40B) "SANDY, SPONGEBOB, AND THE WORM"
Premiere Date: 10/12/01
A gigantic worm attacks Bikini Bottom, so Sandy goes after it. Soon SpongeBob and Sandy are trying to escape the ferocious creature.

41A) "THE ALGAE'S ALWAYS GREENER"
Premiere Date: 3/22/02
Plankton builds a machine that lets him switch lives with Mr. Krabs, so he can have the success (and recipe) he's always wanted.

41B) "SPONGEGUARD ON DUTY"

Premiere Date: 3/22/02
SpongeBob gets a job as a lifeguard . . . and he can't swim!

42A) "CLUB SPONGEBOB"

Premiere Date: 7/12/02
Squidward tries to get into SpongeBob and Patrick's clubhouse, but accidentally propels them into the kelp forest.

42B) "MY PRETTY SEAHORSE"

Premiere Date: 7/12/02
SpongeBob finds a wild seahorse and hides her in the Krusty Krab, where she eats all the Krabby Patties!

43A) "THE BULLY"

Premiere Date: 10/5/01
A bully named Flats terrorizes SpongeBob at boating school . . . until Flats throws a punch and falls down.

43B) "JUST ONE BITE"
Premiere Date: 10/5/01
Squidward finally eats his first Krabby Patty and does everything to keep his new favorite food a secret from SpongeBob.

44A) "NASTY PATTY"
Premiere Date: 3/1/02
SpongeBob and Mr. Krabs think they have killed a health inspector and try to bury him.

44B) "IDIOT BOX"
Premiere Date: 3/1/02
SpongeBob and Patrick use their imaginations to play in an empty box, driving Squidward crazy with their box adventures.

45A) "MERMAIDMAN AND BARNACLEBOY IV"
Premiere Date: 1/21/02
SpongeBob finds Mermaidman's utility belt and accidentally shrinks Squidward and the whole town!

45B) "DOING TIME"
Premiere Date: 1/21/02
SpongeBob and Patrick get entangled with a wanted criminal. They end up driving the criminal so crazy that he turns himself in to the police.

46A) "THE SNOWBALL EFFECT"
Premiere Date: 2/22/02
SpongeBob and Patrick have a snowball fight that escalates into an all-out war with Squidward.

46B) "ONE KRAB'S TRASH"
Premiere Date: 2/22/02
Mr. Krabs sells a worthless hat to SpongeBob, but later finds out it is very valuable.

47A) "AS SEEN ON TV"
Premiere Date: 3/8/02
SpongeBob gets a small part in a Krusty Krab commercial and acts like a spoiled star.

47B) "CAN YOU SPARE A DIME?"
Premiere Date: 3/8/02
Squidward quits the Krusty Krab and moves in with SpongeBob.

48A) "NO WEENIES ALLOWED"
Premiere Date: 3/15/02
SpongeBob has to toughen up to get in the Salty Spittoon, the toughest sailor's club in Bikini Bottom.

48B) "SQUILLIAM RETURNS"
Premiere Date: 3/15/02
Squidward tells Squilliam that he owns a five-star restaurant, and he has to transform the Krusty Krab into a fancy joint, and SpongeBob into a fancy waiter!

49A) "KRAB BORG"
Premiere Date: 3/29/02
After watching a scary movie about robots, SpongeBob convinces Squidward that Mr. Krabs is a robot trying to take over the world.

49B) "ROCK-A-BYE BIVALVE"
Premiere Date: 3/29/02
SpongeBob and Patrick clash as they try to raise a baby clam.

50B) "KRUSTY KRAB TRAINING VIDEO"
Premiere Date: 5/10/02
A training video teaches new employees at the Krusty Krab how things work.

50A) "WET PAINTERS"
Premiere Date: 5/10/02
SpongeBob and Patrick paint Mr. Krabs' house and get paint on Mr. Krabs' first dollar.

51A/B) "SPONGEBOB'S HOUSE PARTY"
Premiere Date: 5/17/02
SpongeBob has a party, but his guests don't have any fun until he gets locked out of his own house.

52A) "CHOCOLATE WITH NUTS"
Premiere Date: 6/1/02
SpongeBob and Patrick sell candy bars door to door and end up buying more than they sell.

52B) "MERMAIDMAN AND BARNACLEBOY V"
Premiere Date: 6/1/02
Barnacleboy is tired of being treated like a child, so he decides to team up with villains Man Ray and the Dirty Bubble.

53A) "NEW STUDENT STARFISH"
Premiere Date: 9/20/02
SpongeBob brings Patrick to boating class and winds up getting detention because of him!

53B) "CLAMS"
Premiere Date: 9/20/02
To celebrate earning his millionth dollar, Mr. Krabs takes SpongeBob and Squidward on a fishing trip.

54A/B) "SPONGEBOB B.C. (BEFORE COMEDY)"
Premiere Date: 3/5/04
It's prehistoric Bikini Bottom, and SpongeGar, Patar, and Squog (SpongeBob, Patrick, and Squidward's Neanderthal alter egos) discover fire!

55A) "THE GREAT SNAIL RACE"
Premiere Date: 1/24/03
SpongeBob trains Gary to race against Squidward's snail, Snellie, in the snail races. Patrick's rock ends up winning.

55B) "MID-LIFE CRUSTACEAN"
Premiere Date: 1/24/03
Mr. Krabs feels old, so when SpongeBob and Patrick announce their night on the town, he wants to tag along.

56A) "BORN AGAIN KRABS"
Premiere Date: 10/4/03
Mr. Krabs eats a spoiled Krabby Patty to prove a point, and the Flying Dutchman comes to escort him to Davy Jones's locker!

56B) "I HAD AN ACCIDENT"
Premiere Date: 10/4/03
SpongeBob breaks his butt while sand sledding and becomes paranoid of all the dangerous things in the outside world, so he holes himself up in his house.

57A) "KRABBY LAND"

Premiere Date: 4/3/04
Mr. Krabs creates a junky playground that kids must pay to use, with the promise that Krabby the Klown will show up to entertain them. When Mr. Krabs turns up short, the kids revolt.

57B) "THE CAMPING EPISODE"

Premiere Date: 4/3/04
Squidward decides to join SpongeBob and Patrick's camping trip . . . in the backyard. Squidward ignores all of their camping advice and ruins the trip.

58A) "MISSING IDENTITY"

Premiere Date: 1/19/04
SpongeBob loses his name tag and finds his mind deteriorating rapidly.

58B) "PLANKTON'S ARMY"

Premiere Date: 1/19/04
Plankton recruits an army of relatives to steal the Krabby Patty Secret Formula. But when they storm the Krusty Krab and get the recipe, Plankton and his army run screaming.

59A/B) "THE SPONGE WHO COULD FLY"

Premiere Date: 3/21/03
SpongeBob attempts to fly with the jellyfish and ends up a laughingstock.

60A) "SPONGEBOB MEETS THE STRANGLER"

Premiere Date: Premiering in the future!
SpongeBob turns the Tattletale Strangler in for littering, and the criminal is determined to get revenge.

60B) "PRANKS A LOT"

Premiere Date: Premiering in the future!
SpongeBob and Patrick turn themselves invisible with invisible spray and they go on a major pranking spree. . . .

The Great SPONGEBOB QUIZ

Are you ready for a quiz? Just how well do you know SpongeBob and the rest of Bikini Bottom? Answers on the next page—NO PEEKING!

1. WHAT IS MR. KRABS'S FULL NAME?

a) Fred C. Krabs

b) Eugene H. Krabs

c) Money H. Krabs

2. WHAT WAS IN THE SMELLY SUNDAE THAT GAVE SPONGEBOB AND PATRICK BAD BREATH?

a) Ketchup, onions, and peanuts

b) Ketchup, garlic, and peanuts

c) Hot fudge, string beans, and tofu

3. WHAT KIND OF TREE DOES SPONGEBOB HAVE IN HIS BATHROOM?

a) Jellyfish tree

b) Peanut tree

c) Christmas tree

4. WHAT IS THE NAME OF THE MOVIE THEATER IN BIKINI BOTTOM?

a) The Sandplex 8
b) Shell Cinema
c) Bikini Bottom Theater
d) The Reef

5. WHO SINGS "LIVING IN THE SUNLIGHT, LOVING IN THE MOONLIGHT"?

a) Big Tim
b) Tiny Tim
c) Medium-Size Tim

6. WHAT DOES SPONGEBOB MAKE SQUIDWARD A SWEATER OUT OF?

a) Seaweed
b) His own eyelashes. Then his tears.
c) Bubbles

You won't find the answers in here!

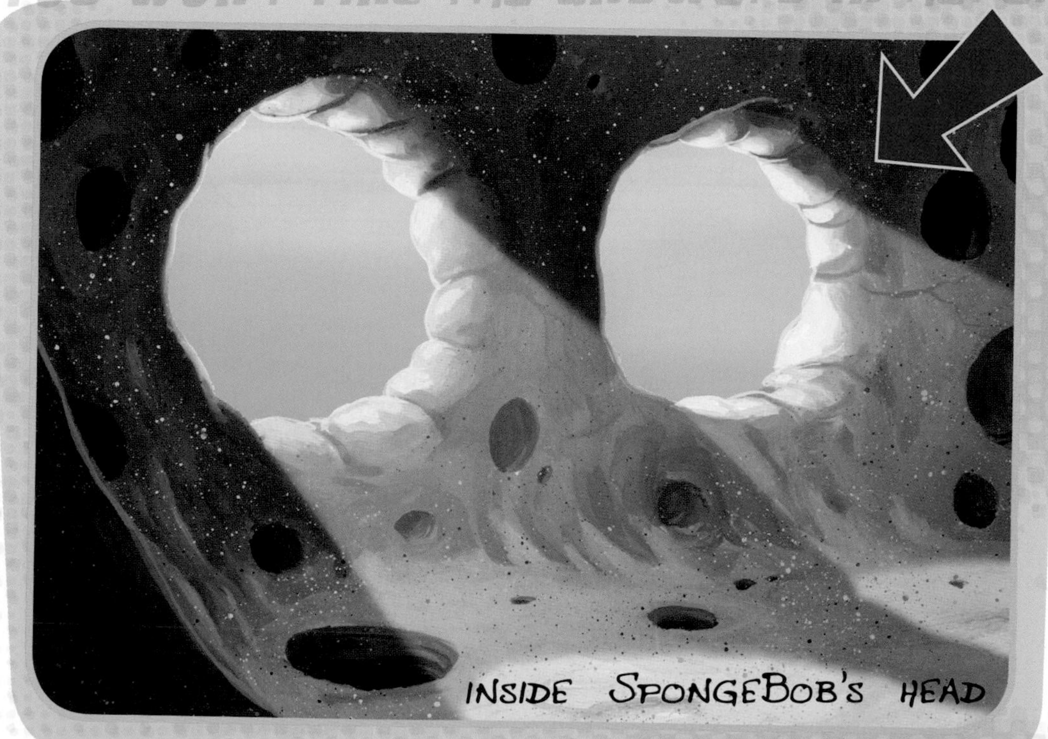

INSIDE SPONGEBOB'S HEAD

7. WHAT IS THE NAME OF THE CUSTOMER WHO COMPLAINED ABOUT NOT HAVING A PICKLE IN HIS KRABBY PATTY?

a) Bubble Bass
b) Bubba Bass
c) Baby Bass

8. WHAT DOES SANDY MAKE FOR SPONGEBOB ON HIS FIRST TRIP TO THE TREEDOME?

a) Fresh-squeezed lemonade
b) Texas tea and cookies
c) Acorn bread

No answers here, either.

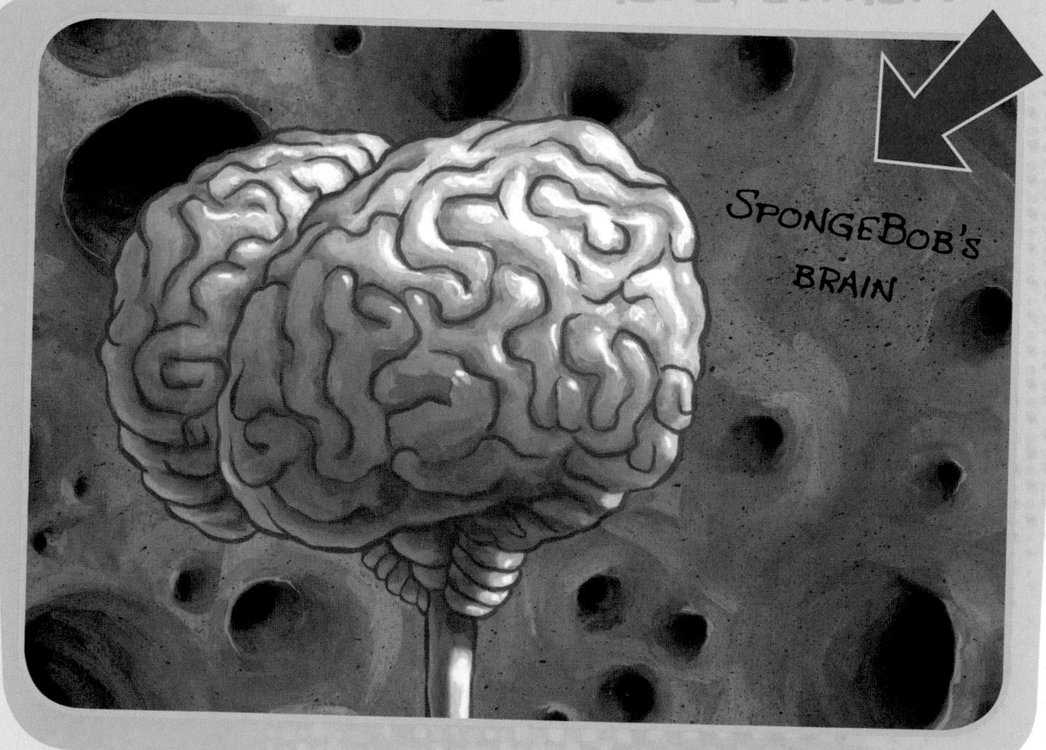

9. WHAT ARE THE MAGIC CONCH'S ANSWERS?

a) No. Yes. Neither. I don't think so. Try asking again. Maybe someday.

b) I don't know. Could be. It's possible. No way, Jose.

c) Could you repeat the question? Not on your life. For sure! Why are you asking me?

10. WHO PLAYS THE REAL-LIFE SEA CAPTAIN IN THE FIRST MERMAIDMAN EPISODE?

a) Don Ho

b) Don Knotts

c) Don the Parking Lot Guy at Nickelodeon Studios

Answers:

1-b, 2-a, 3-b, 4-c, 5-b, 6-b, 7-a, 8-b, 9-b, 10-c

Your SpongeBob Quiz Ratings:

If you answered 0-4 correctly: You call yourself a fan?! I suggest you watch as many *SpongeBob* episodes as you possibly can in order to brush up on your Bikini Bottom knowledge.

If you answered 5-8 correctly: Not bad, but you could use some work. I suggest a steady diet of *SpongeBob* cartoons twice a day.

If you answered 9-10 correctly: You either worked on the show or watch *SpongeBob* twenty-four hours a day! You're a sailorific superfan!

An Exclusive Interview with the One and Only STEPHEN HILLENBURG!

Q: What were some of your favorite cartoons when you were growing up?
Stephen: The Jay Ward cartoons, like *Bullwinkle*. Also Warner Brothers cartoons, *Beany and Cecil*, and *Popeye*.

Q: How much did SpongeBob change from conception to final product?
Stephen: Not much. The essential theme of the show stayed the same: an absurd place underwater. An innocent character who foils the people around him. SpongeBob being naive and innocent stayed the same. We didn't use Pearl as much as I thought we would, but she's more involved with Mr. Krabs.

Q: Are any of the characters based on people you know?
Stephen: Not specific people. A mix of different people. Patrick is like a friend who gets you into a lot of trouble. He's mindless, and it leads you to a crazy situation. Plankton is the only character who's not like a real person, he's more of a caricature.

Q: How did you choose the music for *SpongeBob*?

Stephen: I felt that the Hawaiian music matched the upbeat spirit of SpongeBob. We also used maritime music, Polynesian music, and sea chanteys with accordion. There was a

vaudevillian performer named Roy Smeck in the Twenties and Thirties who played banjo, guitar, steel guitar, and ukulele. We liked his style of music and tried to copy it. He inspired us. I found a lot of the music on one CD from the Sixties by a German-Hawaiian band!

Q: Why does SpongeBob live in a pineapple?

Stephen: I usually tell people it's because he likes the smell. Actually I was sketching ideas for undersea homes made from nautical things like: anchors, rubber boots, ship parts, fish traps, and yes, . . . pineapples. A pineapple seemed to match SpongeBob's personality. It was the brightest and fruitiest.

Q: What are your favorite episodes?

Stephen: It changes all the time. Sometimes I don't like a show. I think we could have improved it, and then I will see it again and it looks good. The first episode that really clicked and felt strong–the animation and characters–was "Ripped Pants." When we got that one back, we wished that they could all be like this! And then I think they got better.

Q: Did you ever work for someone like Mr. Krabs?

Stephen: Yes. He was not cheap, but he was a "salty" guy. He was great. He was the head chef, so I guess that made me SpongeBob.

Q: What would never happen on the show?

Stephen: We would never reveal the secret ingredients of a Krabby Patty. We don't do jokes about popular culture, things that are happening now. It keeps the show and characters timeless. The characters are isolated from the real outside world. It's hard, for example, when SpongeBob had a conversation with TV host Katie Couric, he didn't know who she was.

Q: Why did Mrs. Puff have to pack up and leave her former hometown and move to Bikini Bottom?
Stephen: Who knows? I don't know. It's a secret.

Q: Did you have Ernest Borgnine and Tim Conway in mind when you created Mermaidman and Barnacleboy?
Stephen: No. Nickelodeon wanted celebrity voices. We thought about Bob Denver (Gilligan of *Gilligan's Island*) or someone in a nautical show. We tried to figure out what celebrity would fit. Borgnine and Conway were on the same show, *McHale's Navy*. They were a duo.

ERNEST BORGNINE

TIM CONWAY

Q: Who sings the song at the end of the "Band Geeks" episode?
Stephen: I don't know, but I love it! We were going to use a song like "Stars and Stripes Forever," and someone found this song. It was a happy accident. We used it because it was so wrong, and so right! (The song was sung by David Glen Eisley of the band Giuffria.)

Q: If Gary could talk, what would he say to SpongeBob?
Stephen: Something smart. Gary did talk to him in a dream.

Q: What's the origin of some of the signature phrases on the show like "I'm ready!" and "Bring it around town!"?
Stephen: They totally came out of the moment, out of the writing. We did not consciously try to come up with catch phrases.

Q: According to their driver's licenses, SpongeBob was born in '86 and Mr. Krabs in '42. Do any of the other characters have birth dates?
Stephen: The information on their licenses was in a dream so it really isn't real. SpongeBob is fifty in "sponge years" . . . just kidding. He's old enough to be on his own but still be going to driving school.

Q: Any reason SpongeBob's parents aren't square?
Stephen: I didn't want to put his parents in the show, but Nickelodeon wanted them. I wanted SpongeBob to be the oddest oddball and the "nerdiest" character possible. It would lessen

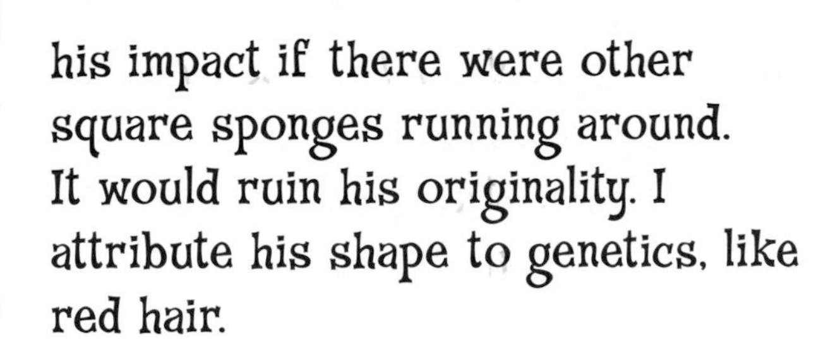

his impact if there were other square sponges running around. It would ruin his originality. I attribute his shape to genetics, like red hair.

Q: How long does it take to create one episode of SpongeBob?
Stephen: About nine months. Sometimes longer when we sit on an idea for a long time before we put it into production.

Q: Do you have a favorite stage of making the show?
Stephen: The writing and drawing is the most fun. Seeing people laugh is always a good reward.

Q: Since you're a surfer, we were wondering if you use a long board or short board?
Stephen: Depends on what kind of shape I'm in, and what kind of day it is. I do both. If the waves are big, I use a short board.

A SECRET REVEALED!

And now, faithful SpongeBob fans, last but not least, what you have all been waiting for . . .

It has never been revealed before!
Guard it with your life!
And DON'T give it to Plankton!

KRABBY PATTY RECIPE

Congratulations! You know how to use a magnifying glass! Did you really think we'd give you the Krabby Patty recipe so easily?

The end.